The Faith of a MELTING GLACIER

AADI H. PANDYA
Illustrations by Blueberry Illustrations

To order additional copies of this book, contact:
Xlibris
1-888-795-4274
www.Xlibris.com
Orders@Xlibris.com

ISBN: Softcover   978-1-7960-8879-3
         Hardcover   978-1-7960-8880-9
         EBook   978-1-7960-8878-6

Library of Congress Control Number: 2020903389

Print information available on the last page

Rev. date: 06/09/2020

I would like to dedicate this book to Jayaba. Jayaba was truly an exceptional human being. Her passion for the environment was very inspirational for me. Her wisdom was endless and I learned so much from her throughout my life. Her enthusiasm at the age of 92 was exemplary. During our trip to Iceland, Jayaba would talk about how beautiful the scenery was and compare it to her home town in India. Despite her age, she participated in every activity and her energy was beyond compare. Even though she wasn't my blood relative, she treated me no differently from her grandchildren. She is always in my thoughts and prayers. May her soul rest in peace.

"John, wake up. It's morning," Mrs. Wiler called as she entered the room, walked to the window, and opened the curtains.

John woke up and squinted as the bright shining light of the early morning sun shone on his face. He yawned and stretched his body.

"Good morning Mom," he greeted.

"Good morning, John. You're going to be late for your trip!"

John looked at the alarm clock on the bed stand. It was 7:30 a.m. He gasped and jumped out of bed. "Oh my god, I overslept."

"Yes, you did. Now hurry up and take a bath. Dad is waiting downstairs to drive you and Robert to the airport."

"Is Robert up yet?"

"Yes, he is finishing his breakfast," Mom replied.

"But, Mom, I haven't even finished packing my bags," John said anxiously.

"Like you ever pack your bags. I already packed them for you. Now go and get ready," she said as she made the bed.

John screamed, "Thank you, Mom," while hurrying into the bathroom.

It was the second week of summer holiday, and John and Robert's parents promised to send them to Iceland to visit Uncle Ben. John and Robert were always amazed each time they saw "giant hills of ice" on TV, and they wished they could see them in real life. Some weeks ago, when they were watching a nature program, they saw big black penguins walking around mighty ice hills, flapping their tiny wings happily.

Robert turned to his dad and asked, "Dad, when can I see one of those ice mountains?"

"Oh, Robert, those are not mountains. They are called glaciers," Dad replied.

"What's a glacier?" asked Robert.

"A glacier is a frozen river that has been on Earth for thousands of years," replied Dad.

"Oh wow! They're really cool. Could you take us to see them?" John requested.

"Yeah, Dad, please can you take us? They look so cool, and I want to see them before school starts," added Robert.

Dad said he would think about it. Both boys were excited. Over the next few days, Robert and John continued pestering their parents, until they finally promised the boys could spend a week with Uncle Ben. Uncle Ben lived in Iceland where there were lots of glaciers.

When John and Robert arrived in Iceland, Uncle Ben was at the airport waiting for them. As they drove down to the small town where Uncle Ben lived, he told them stories about buildings and parks they passed along the way.

The road was very busy. Lots of tourists were coming to the city. Uncle Ben told the boys that Iceland was usually calm and quiet, but during summer, it becomes busy with tourists who wanted to see the glaciers and play on ice.

"Hey, Uncle Ben, I thought Iceland would be colder," wondered Robert.

"Yes, but global warming has caused the temperature to increase. For example, the factory your dad owns produces lots and lots of smoke that goes far up into the sky. This smoke reduces the strength of the shield that protects glaciers from direct sunlight. When this shield is completely gone, there will be nothing up there to protect us from direct sunlight, and the temperature change will be irreversible."

While Uncle Ben was driving, they saw lots of glaciers standing tall like mighty mountains.

"Wow! Uncle Ben, are those glaciers?" John asked, pointing at a huge rock of ice in the distance.

"Yes, they are. Look there's another one," Uncle Ben pointed to another glacier up ahead.

The boys looked and saw many more. They were surrounded by glaciers.

"Wow! They're so big!" Robert said.

"Are they?" Uncle Ben asked.

"They used to be much bigger, but over the last few years, they have been shrinking."

"Are the glaciers losing weight?" John joked. Uncle Ben laughed.

"No, John, the glaciers are getting smaller because of global warming." Uncle Ben tried to explain, but Robert cut in saying,

"Uncle Ben, could you take us to see a glacier right now?" Uncle Ben shook his head.

"No, Robert. I need to take you home now so you can rest after your long flight, but first thing tomorrow, we will go to Skaftafell National Park to see glaciers and icebergs."

The next morning, Robert and John were ready to see the glaciers. They dressed quickly and waited in the living room while Aunt Sally made breakfast.

"Are you ready to go, boys?" Uncle Ben asked as he walked down the stairs.

"Yes, Uncle Ben," the boys echoed.

With that, Uncle Ben drove down to Skaftafell National Park. There were lots of people at the entrance. Many of them held ice skates and hockey sticks. People came in groups to play ice hockey, to snowboard, and to skate down the slippery slopes of ice. Others came with cameras to take pictures of the magnificent glaciers.

When they got inside, the boys were surprised to see how white and foggy and wet everything was. They were shocked to see lots of slush at the base of the glaciers.

"Uncle Ben, what's going on? Why is there so much slush?" John asked sadly.

Uncle Ben shook his head. He did not know that the glaciers had melted this much.

"Uncle Ben, John, look over there," Robert said, pointing to a glacier that was gradually melting. The boys ran to the foot of the melting glacier.

"Oh beautiful glacier, what's happening to you? Why are you melting away?" John asked.

The glacier groaned while a part of it broke off and slowly slid to the ground where it melted like ice cubes dropped onto a hot plate.

Suddenly the glacier started speaking. "Humans have spoiled everything. The world is so warm now, it's making us melt."

The boys were surprised. They stepped back for a moment, and then drew closer.

"I guess you're right," said Robert. "I packed warm clothes but when I got here I realized I didn't need them."

As Robert was speaking, another part of the glacier melted and its water spread around their feet.

"The problem is global warming. Global warming is when the Earth's average temperatures rise. You may not feel it now, but you'll feel it later. We glaciers can feel it, that's why we keep getting smaller and smaller," the disappearing glacier replied.

"But what's causing global warming? What can we do to help you? Please, we don't want you to disappear," John cried.

"Gas combustion from cars and heavy engines and factories fill the air with carbon dioxide and other greenhouse gases. These gases cause global temperatures to rise. Trees are supposed to take in carbon dioxide and release oxygen, but humans keep cutting them down, so carbon dioxide keeps piling up," the glacier said.

"Oh boy," John and Robert said. "What can we do to stop this? We don't want you to disappear."

Once again the glacier couldn't speak. Water covered its mouth. The boys turned to Uncle Ben sadly. "Uncle Ben, what can we do to save the glaciers?" Robert asked.

Another part of the glacier started melting. "Uncle Ben, is it true that gasoline causes the world to heat up?" Robert turned around and asked. He was so confused.

"Yes, I was trying to tell you boys yesterday that the glaciers are getting smaller because of global warming. Apart from burning fuels, agricultural practices like livestock farming also affect the climate. Animals need grassland to graze, which means that forests have to be cleared. When people use sprays that are supposed to help plants grow, the air is filled with greenhouse gases that cause climate change."

The boys nodded as the glacier added, "Your uncle is correct. Earth is surrounded by an atmosphere made up of different layers of gases. When the sun shines, some of its heat enters Earth and keeps it warm enough for us to live in, while some of the heat escapes from the atmosphere. However, due to excessive use of fossil fuels over the years, there is now an abundance of carbon dioxide in the atmosphere. This carbon dioxide traps the extra heat that should have escaped from the atmosphere and causes global warming. That is the reason why we, the glaciers, are melting away."

"There are so many things you can do to help. You can wear a warm sweater when you're cold at home instead of raising the temperature on the heater. Eat more veggies instead of meat. When livestock sellers don't get enough buyers they reduce livestock production and that means forests won't be destroyed. Reduce, reuse and recycle. Instead of throwing broken things away and causing factories to produce new ones, fix and reuse them. Also, always close the door in an air-conditioned room, because when doors are left open, lots of carbon dioxide can escape into the

atmosphere. Always walk or ride a bicycle when you can instead of using a car. Above all, you have to help spread the word. Tell your friends about global warming, and together we can all help save the world."

"But Uncle Ben, you drive a car," John said.

Uncle Ben shook his head. "Yes, I know that's wrong. Starting today, I'll try to ride my bicycle when I'm not going a far distance."

John and Robert turned to the glacier. The water that covered its mouth trickled down to the ground.

"Hey, glacier, can you talk now?" John asked.

"Yeah, the water has stopped trickling for now. This happens to me every few minutes as I start melting. I release about two million gallons of water every five minutes. Soon, I won't even exist," the glacier said.

"Don't worry, glacier. Just hang in there. We will tell all our friends and family about global warming and try to reduce pollution by changing some of our daily routines," assured John. John and Robert left Skaftafell National Park thinking about how they could help save the glaciers.

They spent the rest of their time in Iceland visiting different places and learning more about the effects of global warming. They were shocked to discover the effects of pollution on climate change. The "giant hills of ice" they saw on TV were not going to be around much longer unless something was done. The boys left Iceland determined to do their part to stop global warming and help preserve the glaciers. During the flight back home, they brainstormed ways to begin making changes in their community.

When the boys arrived back home, they went straight to work. They spent hours researching how to reduce pollution, but all the options they found required a great deal of effort and planning, along with the support of many people.

Soon the boys realized they could make a change starting with their father's factory. John and Robert explained the effects of global warming to their dad, and together the three of them made various changes that helped the factory reduce its air pollution. They changed the light bulbs to energy-efficient bulbs, cut down on paper use, and purchased energy-efficient machines. Additionally, both boys became proactive in the community by spending time on the weekends planting trees, recycling garbage, and they even created an organization, the Global Preservation Project (GPP). The focus of this organization was to raise awareness about global warming.

John and Robert knew things wouldn't change overnight. They hoped over time all these small changes would have a big impact on global warming. They had faith that the next time they visit Uncle Ben in Iceland, the glaciers would not be melting as quickly.

While John and Robert were tackling the issues of global warming and pollution, a baby seal waited patiently in the Galapagos Islands for its mother to return.

About the Author

Aadi Pandya is a teenager who is passionate about environmental preservation. He lives in New York with his family and enjoys traveling all over the world. He is often inspired to write about preserving local habitats of the places he visits. Aadi created a non-profit called the Global Preservation Project (GPP). Its main goals are to preserve the environment and to educate people about the world's precious resources. He is also the author of children's books The Faith of a Pink Dolphin and The Faith of a Blue Elephant. You can visit Aadi's organization at www.gppworld.org